for Joe and Mot

Published by Schwartz & Wade Books
an imprint of Random House Children's Books
a division of Random House, Inc. New York

Schwartz & Wade Books and colophon
are trademarks of Random House, Inc.

Visit us on the Web! www.randomhouse.com/kids
Educators and librarians, for a variety of teaching tools,
visit us at www.randomhouse.com/teachers

Library of Congress Cataloging-in-Publication Data
Doughty, Rebecca.
Oh no! Time to go! : a book of goodbyes / by Rebecca Doughty. — 1st ed.
p. cm.
Summary: A young boy presents the different ways his
family members and others say goodbye,
then describes the worst goodbye he ever experienced.
ISBN 978-0-375-84981-7 (hardcover) — ISBN 978-0-375-95696-6 (Gibraltar lib. bdg.)
[1. Stories in rhyme. 2. Farewells—Fiction. 3. Family life—Fiction.] I. Title.
PZ8.3.D743Oh 2009
[E]—dc22
2008022462

The text of this book is set in Belen.
The illustrations are rendered in ink and Flashe paint.
Book design by Rachael Cole

PRINTED IN CHINA
10 9 8 7 6 5 4 3 2 1
First Edition

OH NO! Time to Go!
A Book of Goodbyes

written and illustrated
by Rebecca Doughty

schwartz & wade books · new york

Hi, hey, **HELLO,** I *love* greetings!
The *How are you?*'s at happy meetings.

But then it seems, before you know,
the word's *goodbye*, it's time to go!

My auntie Lou, she says *Yoo-hoo!*
We have a chat, take tea for two,

and when we're through, it's *Toodle-oo, ta-ta, kiss-kiss*, says Auntie Lou.

Uncle Ed has a Southern drawl,
and when he says it, it's *G'bye, y'all.*
It always sounds so sweet and breezy
when Uncle Ed says *Take it easy.*

When Granny comes, it's hugs and kisses,

and when she goes, it's tears and misses.

She says *Later, gator!* and makes me smile,
I say *Back atcha, crocodile!*

And some folks, when it's time to go,
without a word they tell you so.

Instead, they use their hands to say
they really must be on their way.

Dogs have ways to say it too—
a waggy tail says *Howdy-do.*

They lift a leg, or sniff a rear,

a *Grrr!* says *G'won, get outa here!*

Cousin Jazzy, he's one hip cat,
he says *Be cool* and tips his hat.
Gotta split, gotta blow,
see ya, man, I gotta go.

Little brother's just a tot,
can't really talk, sure YELLS a lot.

Goo-goo, ga-ga was all he'd say,

till he shouted out *Bye-bye!* one day.

There's nothing better than hangin' out
with Annabelle and Jake and Scout.

Then suppertime comes, and I yell *NO!*
I won't, I can't, DON'T WANNA GO!

But the *worst* goodbye that I can name
was that *awful* day the movers came!

Don't be a stranger! Promise you'll write!

We watched the van roll out of sight.

There's a *million* ways of saying
words that mean you won't be staying.
But couldn't we just skip the *bye*-ing?

We could stay and keep on *hi*-ing!

Okay, I'll do it. I'll be strong,
but it's *really hard* to say *so long!*

I wish you didn't have to go . . .

. . . but for each **goodbye** . . .

. . . there's a new **hello**.